Three Freckles
Past a Hair

A Grandfather's Legacy of Love

by

P.K. Hallinan

Illustrated by Sally Bourgeois

Forest House Publishing Co., Inc.
Lake Forest, Illinois

FOREST HOUSE ®
Copyright © 1996   Text by P.K. Hallinan
Copyright © 1996   Art by Sally Bourgeois

Published by Forest House Publishing Co., Inc.
P. O. Box 738
Lake Forest, Illinois 60045

Library of Congress Cataloging-in-Publication Data
Hallinan, P. K.
    Three freckles past a hair: a grandfather's legacy of love / P. K.
 Hallinan; illustrated by Sally Bourgeois.
        p.   cm.
    Summary: The special times that he and his grandfather share at
the beach help a young boy cope with his grandfather's death.
        ISBN 1-56674-105-X
    [1. Grandfathers—Fiction. 2. Death—Fiction.] I. Bourgeois,
Sally, ill. II. Title. III. Title: 3 freckles past a hair.
PZ7.H15466Th 1994
[E]—dc20   94–31747
                                                                    CIP
                                                                     AC

ISBN 1-56674-105-X   (Lib. Bndg)
ISBN 1-56674-705-8   (Paperback)
Printed and bound in the United States of America.
1 2 3 4 5 6 7 8 9 R 01 00 99 98 97 96

THREE FRECKLES PAST A HAIR

DEDICATION
IN LOVING MEMORY OF MY FATHER,

KENNETH FRANK HALLINAN
1914 – 1991

who taught me to ride waves
and tell time. Thanks, FLA.

My grandpa was a very different kind of grandfather. He did lots of crazy things, which I loved. For example, he always cooked his bacon east to west. That's because he believed that if you cooked it north to south it would bring bad luck.

6

Also, he didn't like to see Daylight Savings Time end, so he always refused to change his clocks back. I worried about this. I was sure that Grandpa would get into trouble with the U.S. government. But he never did. The only person who got into trouble was Gran, my grandmother, who could never figure out what time it was and kept arriving at all of her appointments either two hours early or two hours late.

Grandpa's greatest love, besides Gran, was the ocean. He loved to bodysurf, which he did every single day, rain or shine, month in and month out, for as long as I could remember.

And so, every single day, rain or shine, month in and month out, Grandpa and I would walk down to the beach together. We always wore our hats. We always carried our folding beach chairs with our towels stuck inside. We always wore our baggy orange swim trunks. And we always listened to the raspy whish of our rubber flip-flops, as we shuffled along the concrete sidewalk, that led to the sea.

Everyone knew Grandpa, especially the local surfers
who would shout and wave as we walked by. "Hey, Gramps!
Surf's up!" Grandpa knew, or pretended to know, all of them.
But I don't think he ever learned any of their names.

Gramps was not good with names. He said that learning names was too much like work. So he just waved back and made a seal-like barking sound, which they greatly enjoyed.

On the beach, we always sat in the same spot at the foot of the long, sandy ramp that the lifeguards used for their jeeps. We'd line up our towels side by side, put our beach chairs behind them, then sit down and wait. We always waited for about an hour before Grandpa went bodysurfing. He didn't like to go into the water until it was exactly three freckles past a hair.

I never really knew how Grandpa told time. All I know, is that eventually, he would look at his wrist and announce that it was three freckles past a hair. Then he'd stand up, cinch his baggy orange swim trunks by pulling on the white strings, and head into the ocean.

And he ALWAYS shuffled his feet. This was to tell the dangerous stingrays that he was coming. Grandpa had stepped on several stingrays and he liked to give them every chance to leave.

Once in the water, Grandpa would ride the waves like a porpoise.

Sometimes he'd glide to the left.

Sometimes he'd glide to the right.

And sometimes, he'd glide right down the middle of the wave and perform his patented "Grandpa Barrel Roll," which he'd learned in his days as a test pilot.

He'd ride each wave until the wave was gone and then race back out to catch the next one. He loved to bodysurf.

When Grandpa was done in the water, he'd walk back to his chair and dry his face with his towel. Then we'd take a long walk down to the pier.

Our walks were always slow and enjoyable. It was important to notice how the seagulls all faced the sun, but it was even more important to remember to touch the pier at the end of each walk, because if you didn't, the walk didn't count.

Sometimes we'd walk beyond the pier, and this is when Grandpa would use his extraordinary eyesight to read the clock on the tower, about a mile away.

"What time does the clock say?" I would ask, and grandpa would answer, "It's ten till two." Of course, the clock had been broken for years and always read ten till two. But it was still amazing that he could see that far. I know I couldn't.

And this is what we did every single day, rain or shine, month in and month out.

Then one day it was over.

I went to Grandpa's house with my hat on my head, my
towel stuffed into my beach chair, and my flip-flops
whishing with each step.

But when Gran answered the door, I could tell by her face something was wrong.

She stood in front of me wringing her hands. She told me that Grandpa was very sick. He was in bed and he wouldn't be able to go bodysurfing today.

Then she asked me if I'd like
to visit with him. I said, "yes."
Grandpa looked pale, but he greeted me with
a weak version of his seal-like barking sound.

I sat down by his bed and we talked. All he wanted to know was what kind of day it was and what the surf looked like. I said that it was a beautiful day and that the surf was perfect. He smiled at that and settled back against his pillow. Then he asked me to leave. He said he needed to sleep.

So I tiptoed quietly away.

And I knew, as I left, that Grandpa was never coming down to the beach again.

I went to the beach by myself that day. I sat where Grandpa and I always sat, at the foot of the sandy ramp, that the lifeguards used for their jeeps. And I watched the waves and imagined Grandpa

gliding to the left,

then gliding to the right,

then occasionally gliding right down the middle of the wave, performing his patented "Grandpa Barrel Roll," that he'd learned in his days as a test pilot.

A little while later, I took a walk down to the pier,
touching it, of course, so that the walk would count. I
then went beyond, all the way to the tower, about a mile
away. It was during my walk that Grandpa passed
away, at exactly ten till two.

Grandpa was buried at sea, in his beloved ocean,
as had been his wish. Gran was very brave, but I could tell
that her loss was even greater than mine. She had been with
Grandpa for over 50 years and now her lifelong companion
was gone. We both found comfort, however, in the knowledge
that Grandpa was forever in his favorite place on earth.

25

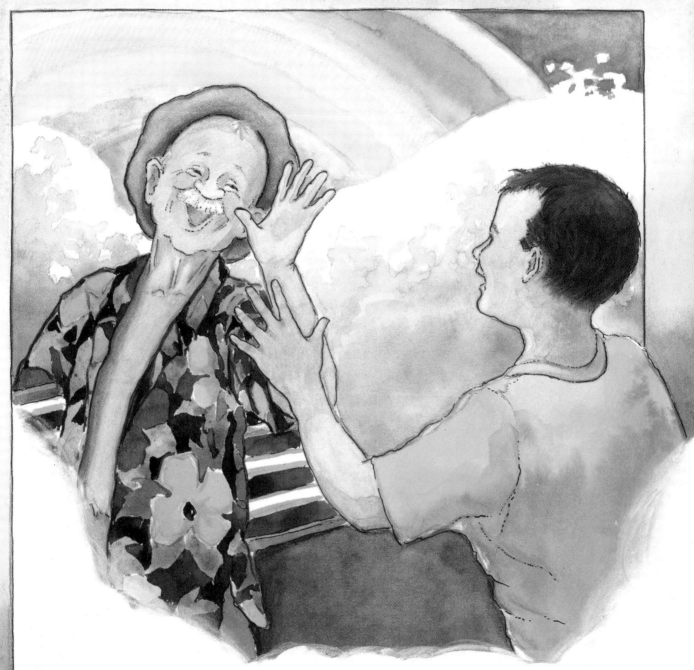

The next day, I again went down to the beach and sat in our usual spot. I was quite sad. I wanted to have Grandpa next to me, and I missed him.

As I sat there, I wondered where Grandpa really was, and if he was happy. I imagined him wandering around heaven, waving at people and making his seal-like barking sound, and I smiled.

"Grandpa," I said looking up at the sky, " if you have a moment, please send me a sign so I can know you're truly happy now."

I sat there for about an hour, studying the waves and imagining Grandpa gliding down them. Then I stood up, cinched in my baggy orange swim trunks by pulling on the white strings, and began shuffling toward the sea. That's when I saw the porpoise.

The porpoise was large and silvery gray, and had a huge dark fin that sliced noiselessly in and out of the water.

29

When the porpoise was directly in front of me, it suddenly turned towards me and gleefully began riding the waves. First it glided to the left. Then it glided to the right. And then it glided right down the middle of the wave and performed the patented "Grandpa Barrel Roll." This surprised me, because I thought that only test pilots knew how to do this.

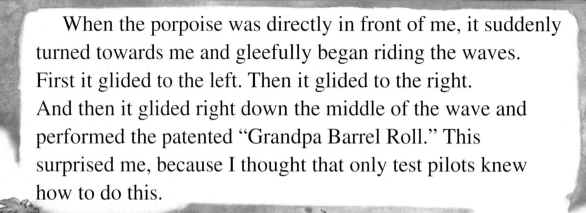

The porpoise happily rode each wave until the wave was gone and then raced back out to catch the next one. He loved to bodysurf.

As I watched him both in amazement and with curiosity, I checked the time by looking at my wrist.

It was exactly three freckles past a hair.